THE TWENTY-SEVENTH ANNUAL AFRICAN HIPPOPOTAMUS RACE

Morris Lurie
Illustrated by Richard Sawers

SIMON AND SCHUSTER · NEW YORK

For Ben,

Future Champion

Text copyright © 1969 by Morris Lurie
Illustrations copyright © 1969 by Richard Sawers
Published in the United States by Simon and Schuster, Children's Book Division
Rockefeller Center, 630 Fifth Avenue
New York, New York 10020

First U.S. Printing

SBN 671-65105-6 Trade
SBN 671-65104-8 Library
Library of Congress Catalog Card Number: 78-82774
Printed in Great Britain

j L 974 tw

CHAPTER ONE

Into The River

When Edward Day turned eight years old, his mother put him on the scales to see how much he weighed, and his father measured him with a tape measure to see how big he was, and then his grandfather took a photograph of him with the old family camera, and everyone was happy with the way Edward was growing up. He weighed two and a half tons, he was four feet high and eleven feet long, and he was a lovely grey in colour. His eyes were small and bulgy, and his mouth was huge. He didn't have a hair on his head, but that was all right, because hippopotamuses never do, and Edward was a hippopotamus.

"I'm going for a swim!" cried Edward, and dived into the river which flowed past the family back garden.

"Doesn't he swim well?" said his mother (whose name was Milly).

"Like a fish," said his grandmother (whose name was Prunella).

"Nonsense!" exclaimed his grandfather (whose name was Theodore). "He swims like a hippopotamus. A fish? Never!

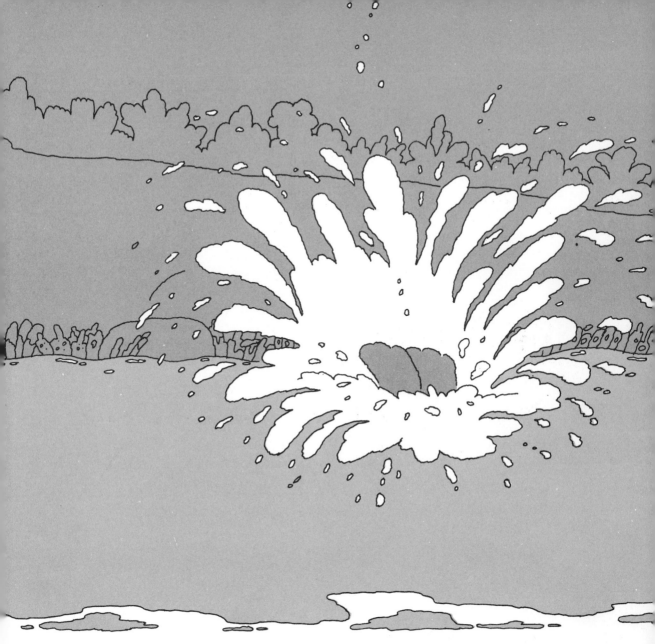

Can a fish dive like that? Can a fish run along the bottom like that? Can a fish jump out of the water and run along the bank as fast as a man? Can a fish sink like a rock and float like a log? Only a hippopotamus can do that, and Edward can do all those things better than any other hippopotamus I have ever seen. Mark my words," said Edward's grandfather, "Edward has a great future ahead of him."

"That's my hippo," said Edward's father (whose name was

Sam), putting a fresh cigar between his teeth and proudly watching Edward as he swam down the river. Edward's father was a sporty gentleman, who liked tweed hats and check coats, and was very interested in racing.

Indeed, Edward *was* a very good swimmer. He wasn't exceptionally smart at school – though he tried very hard – and he wasn't brilliant at games, but in the water. . .

At quarter speed, he looked like a log shooting down a fast stream.

At half speed, he looked like a powerful motor boat.

At full speed, you could hardly see him at all.

"Whoosh!" went Edward, diving down to the bottom.

Yes, Edward was fast. Why, only a week before his eighth birthday, he had won first place in the big local swimming race, beating every other hippopotamus in the neighbourhood.

"Thank you very much," Edward said, when he had won that race, and everyone was crowded around him. "Thank you very much. Very kind of you. Actually, I think I was lucky. I got into a fast bit of the river, that's all."

When Edward turned eight years old, and he had been weighed and measured and photographed, and come in from his swim, his grandfather put his arm around his shoulders, and said to him, "Edward, my boy, how would you like to win the Twenty-Seventh Annual African Hippopotamus Race?"

"Gosh!" said Edward. "Me?"

"Edward," said his grandfather, "I have seen some fast hippopotamuses in my time, as you know, and I think you've got the makings of a champion."

"Gosh!" said Edward. "Me?"

"Yes, Edward," said his grandfather. "You can do it. Prunella. Fetch me the map."

Edward's grandmother ran upstairs to get the map, and while they were waiting, all Edward could say was, "Gosh! Gosh!"

The Twenty-Seventh Annual African Hippopotamus Race!

"Here's the map," said Edward's grandmother, panting a little from her run up the stairs.

"Hmmm," said Edward's grandfather, spreading the map out over the dining table. "Let me see. Ah. Edward," he said, "this is the Zamboola River." He pointed with his finger.

Edward blinked. Running right across the map was a wide band of blue, and on it was written *Zamboola River*.

"The Zamboola River," said Edward's grandfather, "is the longest, widest, deepest river in all Africa. A treacherous and dangerous river. A hard river to swim. Unless you know what you're doing."

"Gosh!" said Edward, blinking furiously.

"Over here," said Edward's grandfather, pointing with his finger, "are swamps. And over here is a waterfall. But in between are fourteen miles of clear, blue water, and that's where the race is held."

"Fourteen miles?" said Edward. "Fourteen miles?"

"It's a long race, Edward," said Edward's grandfather, "but you can do it. Mind you, you'll have to train very hard. No cakes! No sweets! A strict racing diet. You'll have to give up playing with your friends and devote all your time to swimming, swimming, nothing but swimming. The champion's road is hard and lonely, but the rewards at the end are great."

"But what about school?" asked Edward's mother. Proud though she was of her son's swimming prowess, she tended to worry about him being in the water so often.

"Oh, there'll be time for school," said Edward's grandfather.

Edward's head went round and round. Ever since he could remember, he had been told tales of the Annual African Hippopotamus Race.

Just the thought of it made him gulp. His stomach began to quiver with the jitters. All those champion hippopotamuses! And every hippopotamus in Africa – and hundreds of other animals as well – standing along the banks, waving and cheering!

"Is this the Zamboola River?" said Edward's grandmother, peering at the map. "Why, it's only fourteen inches long. Anyone can swim that."

"Prunella," said Edward's grandfather, "that's a map, not the real river."

"Oh," she said, fidgeting with her spectacles and peering even closer at the map. "It looks like fourteen inches to me."

"Well, Edward?" said Edward's grandfather. "Naturally,"

he added, "I will be your trainer."

Edward beamed with joy. To be trained by his grandfather!

"Gosh!" he said.

For Edward's grandfather wasn't just an ordinary hippopotamus. In his time, he had been a champion hippopotamus. He had come third in the Fourth Annual African Hippopotamus Race, many years before.

"What do you say, son?" said Edward's father.

"Well," said Edward, knowing that he had to make a decision, "if you think I have a chance – and you really don't mind spending all your time training me – I'd love to try for the race."

"I knew it!" cried Edward's grandfather. "I knew it all along! I knew Edward was going to be a champion, the minute he was born. Of course I don't mind training you. It's an honour. Well, let's not stand around. Into the river!"

CHAPTER TWO

Six Days To Go

Every morning, when it was still dark and ordinary hippo-potamuses were still asleep, with the sky like velvet and the stars just starting to go out, Edward leapt from his bed, out of his pyjamas and into his bathing trunks. Wasting not a second, looking to neither left nor right, he ran for the river at the end of the garden, and dived in.

Splash!

First he swam five miles down the river, going as fast as he could. Then he flipped over and came all the way back, trying to go even faster. His little bulgy eyes were closed tight – except for an occasional fast look just to make sure he was going in the right direction – while his huge mouth was open one minute, closed the next, sucking up enormous breaths. Over and over went his arms, cleaving a pathway through the water. And with each stroke of an arm, he gave a powerful kick with a leg.

Whoosh! Whoosh!

And no sooner was he back at the garden than he leapt out and immediately began twenty minutes of vigorous exer-cises, touching his toes, running on the spot, windmills, press-ups, deep knee bends and two-legged leaps.

"One! Two! One! Two!" he chanted as he worked.

By the time he had finished all these, his grandfather was up, and he gave Edward a massage with alcohol, to keep his muscles supple and loose.

And then, when that was done, Edward put on his dressing gown and sat down to breakfast with the rest of the family.

"How did it go, Champ?" Edward's father asked him. Ever since Edward had started training for the Twenty-Seventh Annual African Hippopotamus Race, his father had taken to calling him "Champ".

"Terrific!" Edward said. "I feel fine."

And how hungry he was after all that exercising. Six eggs! Four glasses of milk! Ten pieces of toast, each piece thickly buttered and covered with marmalade.

"Watch that diet, Champ," his father said.

"Quickly, now," said Edward's mother. "It's time for school."

And Edward had just enough time to change into his

school clothes, put his books into his school bag, and run off.

Back he came at twelve o'clock, when school finished for the day, and hippopotamuses went home for lunch and to sleep in the afternoon – a very sensible thing to do when it's hot.

His grandfather allowed Edward only one hour's sleep – most hippopotamuses have three or four – and then training began again.

This time, when Edward dived into the river, his grand-

father jumped on to a bicycle, and as Edward swam down the river, his grandfather bicycled along the bank, shouting out instructions through a megaphone.

"Keep your head down! Keep your head down! Use your legs! Use your legs!"

He shouted everything twice, because he knew it was hard to hear when you were swimming fast with your eyes shut tight and your mouth opening and closing, sucking up enormous quantities of air.

"Push with that left leg! Push with that left leg!" he shouted, bicycling along the bank, his legs flying on the pedals.

"That'll do! That'll do! Come out! Come out! Take a rest. Whew! You're too fast for me."

Poor old Theodore. It was a long time since he'd done anything as strenuous as bicycling up and down a river bank, shouting instructions through a megaphone. He felt a bit wobbly in the legs.

"How's it going, Champ?" said Edward's father, who had come down to the river to see how Edward was making out.

"Fine!" said Edward. "I feel terrific."

"He's too fast for me," said Edward's grandfather. "I'm out of breath. Just a minute. Lots to do. Lots to do. Lotssssss. . ."

Edward's grandfather was asleep.

But an hour later he was back again, as keen as ever.

"Now, Edward," he said, "back into the river. This time I'm going to time you with my stop watch. I want you to swim three miles, up to that tree, as fast as you can. Ready? On your mark! Go!"

That night, when Edward's training was over for the day, when he had had his shower, put on a clean pair of pyjamas, eaten his supper, checked his homework to make sure it was all ready for the next day at school, and was in his bed, fast asleep, Edward's grandfather sat down at the family desk, took out a sheet of paper and an envelope, unscrewed his fountain pen, and, very carefully, wrote a letter to the President of the Twenty-Seventh Annual African Hippopotamus Race.

"Dear President," he wrote. *"I would like to enter my grandson Edward in the Twenty-Seventh Annual African*

Hippopotamus Race. His vital statistics are as follows: he is four feet and one half inch high. He is eleven feet and two inches long. His weight is two and a half tons, three pounds and five ounces. His age: eight last birthday. I believe him to be a true champion, but that you will be able to judge for yourself. He is being trained by yours truly."

And here he signed his name.

There!

And so the days went, each day beginning with the *buzz-buzz* of Edward's alarm clock.

Into the river!

And there was so much to learn.

One afternoon, Edward's grandfather began to show Edward how to do a proper racing dive.

"Head down! Head down!" he called. "On your mark! On your mark!"

Edward tucked his head down, the way he had been shown. Up went his arms. He hooked his toes over the edge of the riverbank, for extra leverage. He took a deep breath, and held it. He leant forward, and waited for the signal to dive in.

Seconds passed. Edward, tense as a spring, waited and waited. Where was the signal?

"Oh!" cried Edward, who could lean forward no longer, and before he could help himself, in he toppled.

Splash!

Up shot a huge wave of water, waking up Edward's grandfather.

"What happened?" said Edward's grandfather. "Oh. Oh. I fell asleep."

"Do you want me to try it again?" asked Edward.

"Um," said Edward's grandfather, who still felt sleepy. "No. This time I want you to swim five miles down the river, and five miles back. As fast as you can. Ready? Go!"

And while Edward was swimming down the river as fast as he could, Edward's grandfather lay down under a shady tree and took a nap. Edward's training really was taking it out of him. It was a long time since he had had to do so much.

But Edward's father, taking a stroll along the river bank,

cigar in mouth, woke him up.

"Have you seen the paper?" he said. "Look at this. Seems there are going to be a record number of entries this year."

"Wait till I get my spectacles," said Edward's grandfather. "There. Let me see. Ah. Um. *Record number of entries.* Mmm. *Thirty-eight hippopotamuses have so far entered in the Twenty-Seventh Annual African Hippopotamus Race.* Well, well. Very interesting."

Meanwhile, Edward's grandmother was sitting under a shady tree, knitting a pair of racing trunks, navy blue in colour, with a white belt, all pure wool, for Edward to wear for the Twenty-Seventh Annual African Hippopotamus Race. Click, click went her knitting needles, as the racing trunks took shape.

On and on went Edward's training.

He loved all of it.

Except for one thing.

There were his school friends, playing games and going for snoozes, doing anything they wanted to do, and here he was, swimming up and down the river, up and down, up and down.

How long it was since he had played games with his friends!

One day, when he was feeling very low, who should come crashing through the reeds to watch him swim but Humphrey and Tad, William and Jeffrey, Benjamin and Luke, his very best friends.

"That's the style, Edward!" they cried, cheering and waving. "You show them! Hooray! Hooray!"

Edward felt so happy, seeing all his friends, and hearing them clapping and shouting encouragement, that he struck out in the river, going faster than ever before, so fast that his grandfather, who was on his bicycle, fell right behind and finally gave up altogether and came to rest alongside a tree.

"That hippopotamus is the fastest I've ever seen," said Edward's grandfather. "He's faster than me. And I'm on a bicycle."

One day, when Edward climbed out of the river, after a gruelling five mile swim, there was his father, on the river bank.

"A letter's just arrived," said Edward's father. "It's for Theodore."

They had to wait till Edward's grandfather came panting up on his bicycle.

The envelope was blue, the colour of the sky, and in the top right hand corner was a stamp, and in the top left hand corner was a drawing of a hippopotamus, barely an inch long, drawn in gold.

"It's from the President of the Twenty-Seventh Annual African Hippopotamus Race," said Edward's grandfather.

"Dear Sir," he read. *"We are pleased indeed to accept your grandson Edward for the Twenty-Seventh Annual African Hippopotamus Race. The race will be held, as it is held every year, on the First of June. I look forward to seeing you and your grandson on that date. Best Wishes. Good Luck. Yours Sincerely, The President of the Twenty-Seventh Annual African Hippopotamus Race."*

"Gosh!" said Edward, blinking his eyes and breathing rapidly through his huge mouth, which had fallen wide open. "Six days to go!"

CHAPTER THREE

The Yellow Bus

Six days to go!

And how quickly they flew.

Edward started training twice as hard. Instead of five miles, he swam ten. Instead of twenty minutes of exercises, he did forty.

Meanwhile, Edward's father was preparing the yellow bus.

For many years, Edward's father had been looking for a suitable vehicle for the family. He needed something extra big, because there were five in his family. Nothing that Edward's father saw seemed right. Then one day he took a trip to London, and there he saw exactly what he needed.

A red double-decker bus!

He didn't like the colour much, but everything else was right, so he bought himself a red double-decker bus and put it on the ship to take home.

"I'll paint it yellow," he thought. "Yellow is a much happier colour."

When he got the bus back to Africa, he set about painting it. As soon as that was done, he took out all the seats. Then he decided to take out all the upstairs part, including the stairs.

"Ah, much better!" he thought, when he had done all that.

Now there was nothing inside the bus but the steering wheel, the brake, and the pedals.

"To work, to work!" said Edward's father.

He covered the walls with striped orange and green wallpaper, carefully avoiding covering up the windows.

He hung up an enormous glittering crystal chandelier.

He put in a big comfortable seat for the driver, and, behind it, a big comfortable seat for passengers.

In the back of the bus, he put in a big comfortable bed.

On the top of the bus he put a flagpole, and now, with Edward in his last days of training, Edward's mother sewed a flag, as big as a bed sheet. It was bright yellow, the same colour as the bus, and on it, there was just one word: *Edward*.

No sooner was the flag hoisted to the top of the flagpole than Edward's grandfather, who had been consulting his calendar, announced, "One day to go! One day to go! Training has ceased! Training has ceased!"

"Gosh!" said Edward. "One day to go! I'd better train twice as hard!"

"No," said Edward's grandfather, laying aside the megaphone and wheeling away his bicycle, "training has ceased." You don't want to overtrain. That's fatal. All you have to do now is relax. Tonight you'll have a good, deep, restful, relaxing sleep. Your training is complete."

"Your bed's all ready in the yellow bus," said Edward's mother.

"And here are your navy blue racing trunks," said Edward's grandmother. "Finished just in time."

"We're all coming along to the Zamboola River," said Edward's father. "And I'm driving," he added proudly.

Edward noticed that his father was wearing a new hat, a really snappy hat with a little flag stuck into the band on one side. And on the little flag was one word: *Edward*.

"Where are you sitting in the bus?" Edward asked his

grandfather.

"I'm sitting on the back seat, with Grannie," said Edward's grandfather. "Your mother is sitting beside her, behind the driver, who happens to be your father. Now run along and see your friends. I'm sure they'll be pleased to see you, after all this time."

So Edward ran off to see Humphrey and Tad, William and Jeffrey, Benjamin and Luke, his closest and best friends, whom he hadn't played with since his training had begun.

"We're all coming too," they told him. "Every hippopotamus in the neighbourhood is coming. We want to be there to see you win."

"That's wonderful!" cried Edward. "I'll swim better than ever now, knowing you'll all be there."

That afternoon, for the first time in months, Edward played with his friends. They played football, all of them bellowing and roaring happily, and then they went for a snooze on a sandbank.

When, at last, it was time for Edward to go home, he felt completely relaxed and at peace with the world.

"Supper is ready," said his mother. "Eat up, then brush your teeth, and then into bed."

"And when you wake up tomorrow morning," said Edward's father, "we'll be at the Zamboola River.

CHAPTER FOUR

The Mighty Zamboola

All night long, Edward's father drove the yellow bus. And how much traffic there was on the road! Everyone – every hippopotamus in Africa – was going to the Twenty-Seventh Annual African Hippopotamus Race at the Zamboola River.

There were cars and trucks, bicycles and scooters, buses and vans, carts, lorries, caravans, motor bikes and tractors. Their lights swarmed like glow worms in the night.

But Edward, of course, saw none of this. He was fast asleep, in the big comfortable bed, in the back of the yellow bus. The glittering crystal chandelier had been switched off. Curtains had been drawn over all the rear windows. Edward's father drove as carefully as he could, avoiding all bumps, so that his son would have a deep, relaxing, refreshing, undisturbed sleep.

As the sun was coming up, they neared the Zamboola River.

"Get a good parking spot," said Edward's mother.

"Who's driving this bus?" said Edward's father, wiggling his cigar about in his mouth. "Leave it to me. I know just the place."

He turned off the main road, drove for a time along a quiet path, and at last came to a stop.

"How's this, love?" he said to his wife, pulling on the hand brake.

"Sam, it's wonderful!" cried his wife.

And it was. They were on the top of a hill. Below them, the land fell away, and at the bottom of the hill, lay the Zamboola River.

It was just the way it appeared on the map, with the swamp at one end, the waterfall at the other, and, in between, fourteen miles of deep, wide river.

"Five minutes' walk," said Edward's father. "Downhill all the way."

An hour later, Edward, in the big comfortable bed in the back of the yellow bus, opened his eyes.

The first thing he noticed was that the bus was no longer moving.

The second thing he noticed was that there was a delicious smell of hot pancakes in the air.

He leapt out of his bed, drew back the curtains, and there before his small bulgy eyes (which were blinking so fast you could hardly see them) was the most fabulous sight he had ever seen in his life.

Hippopotamuses! Rhinoceroses! Elephants! Giraffes! Water buffalos! Monkeys! And a sky filled with birds!

"Gosh!" said Edward.

There were millions of animals, more than he had ever seen together, in the one place, in his whole life. And that was just the beginning.

There were flags.

Thousands of flags!

There were umbrellas.

Thousands of umbrellas!

There were balloons.

There were streamers.

All these things, as far as he could see.

Edward was speechless. He felt giddy and dizzy with nervousness and excitement, but, at the same time, he couldn't take his eyes away from the fabulous sight.

Just then, the door at the back of the yellow bus flew open, and there were his mother, and his father, and his grandmother, and his grandfather, all beaming with joy.

"Good morning, Edward!" they cried. "Isn't it a fabulous sight? Isn't it a wonderful day? Isn't it the best thing you've ever seen in your whole life?"

"Gosh!" cried Edward. "Gosh! Gosh! Gosh! Gosh!"

"How do you feel, Champ?" asked Edward's father. "Have a good sleep? Bet you didn't even know we were moving."

"Come along, Edward," cried Edward's mother. "It's time for breakfast. We're having your favourite food. Pancakes."

"Pancakes!" cried Edward. His face lit up with joy. "They're my favourite food."

And, wasting no time, he sat himself down at the fold-up table which Edward's father had set up under a shady tree, tucked a napkin into the front of his dressing gown, and picked up his knife and fork, all ready to start.

"Where's Grandfather?" asked Edward, noticing he wasn't there.

"Coming, coming!" cried a voice from inside the yellow bus, and a few seconds later, out ran Edward's grandfather.

"Something I want to show you, boy," he said, sitting down opposite Edward at the table. "First thing I did, while you were still asleep, was run down to the river. Very important. Have to check up on river temperature, current flow, things like that. And here it is," he said, placing before Edward a small glass jar with a screw-top lid, and inside the jar something that looked like water. "The mighty Zamboola!"

CHAPTER FIVE

Eighty-Four Champions

Breakfast was over. It was nine o'clock. The sky was a faultless blue.

"Right, Edward," said Edward's grandfather. "Let's go down and see the President."

"What time is the race?" asked Edward. He was feeling much better now, not quite so jittery and nervous and excited, having had his favourite breakfast of hot, golden pancakes, and six glasses of cold, creamy milk to go with them.

"The Annual African Hippopotamus Race," said Edward's grandfather, "is always held at the same time. Four o'clock in the afternoon."

"Lunch will be ready at twelve o'clock," said Edward's mother. "Don't be late."

All the way down the hill, all the way to the President's tent, hippopotamuses waved to Edward. "Good luck!" they cried. "Good swimming!"

"Gosh!" said Edward. "I don't know all these hippopotamuses, do I?"

"No," said Edward's grandfather, "but they know you. Your name has been in the newspaper, and your photograph too."

"Gosh!" said Edward. "I didn't know that."

It was so sunny and glary outside (even with dark glasses on), that when Edward stepped inside the President's tent, for a few moments he couldn't see anything at all.

It was so dark and so huge.

"This way, Edward," said Edward's grandfather.

The tent seemed to be filled with hippopotamuses. Some had cameras and were taking photographs. Some were writing on pads and in books. And some were just standing there. But everyone was talking, and the noise was terrific.

"This is my grandson, Edward," Edward heard his grand-father saying. "Take off your glasses, Edward. This is the President of the Twenty-Seventh Annual African Hippo-potamus Race."

Edward took off his glasses and blinked. He was standing in front of a long, low table, with his grandfather on one side of him, and his father on the other, and right along the table, across from him, were fifteen old hippopotamuses, all sitting on small silver chairs. All, that is, except for the hippopotamus he was now being introduced to. He was on a gold chair.

"Good morning, Edward," he said, offering Edward his hand.

The President! He was the oldest, grandest hippopotamus Edward had ever seen.

"Good morning, Sir," said Edward.

The President's face was lined with age, but his hand was steady and hard. There was something noble about him, about the way his head rode on his broad shoulders, about the way he sat, so straight and yet at ease. He was the most wonderful hippopotamus Edward had ever seen.

"And how are you, Theodore?" the President asked Edward's grandfather. "Keeping fit? You're looking well. I saw your grandfather racing in the Fourth Annual African Hippopotamus Race," the President said to Edward, "and he swam a fine race. A real champion. Now, Edward," said the President. "All I want you to do is sign your name here, and then you're an Official Entrant. Here, use my pen."

Edward signed his name with great care to the long scroll of paper which the President placed before him, and then handed back the pen.

"This way, my boy," said Edward's grandfather. "Lots to do, lots to do!"

"Isn't the President a wonderful hippopotamus!" said Edward.

"He was the winner of the First Annual African Hippopotamus Race," said Edward's grandfather. "Twenty-seven years ago. A real champion."

No sooner had Edward left the President's table, than a hippopotamus with a camera came up to him.

"May I have your photograph, please?" he asked Edward. "I'm from the newspaper."

Then up came a reporter, pad in hand.

"No time for interviews now," said Edward's grandfather. "Plenty of time for him later. Come along. Come along."

"Don't worry, Edward," said Edward's father. "I'll give the reporter all the facts. You go along with your grandfather."

And Edward's father applied a match to his cigar (which had gone out), pushed his hat back, and began to give the reporter all the facts, while the reporter scribbled them down in his pad as fast as he could, and Edward and his grandfather went off to the weighing machine.

"Every champion has to be weighed before a race," said Edward's grandfather. That's the rule. Now, step behind that screen and take off your clothes. I'll wait here."

Edward stepped behind the screen and took off his clothes, hung them up carefully on the hook provided, and then stepped out again, feeling slightly funny with no clothes on.

But then he saw that there were quite a few hippopotamuses with no clothes on. How strange that he hadn't noticed them before.

And what magnificent hippopotamuses they were! Each one looked strong and firm and solidly muscled and perfectly trained. And how confident they all looked! There was one who must have weighed at least a ton more than Edward! And there was another, with *superb* muscles!

Edward gulped.

In all the time that he had been training, he had never once thought of other hippopotamuses. His only concern had been to follow his grandfather's instructions, and to swim as well as he could. And now, seeing all these other hippopotamuses, he felt very nervous indeed.

"Gosh!" said Edward to his grandfather. "Look at all these champions!"

"Don't worry about them," said Edward's grandfather. "Let's see what they look like in the water."

"Well . . ." said Edward.

"Come along," said a hippopotamus in a white coat. "Hop on the scales. You're next."

"Oh!" said Edward, and stepped on to the scales.

"Name?" said the hippopotamus in the white coat.

"Edward," said Edward.

"Hmm," said the hippopotamus in the white coat, and he wrote Edward's name down in a book.

Edward saw that the hippopotamus who was weighing him had a small round badge on the label of his white coat, and on the badge was written *Official*.

"Now, breathe out," said the Official hippopotamus to Edward. "Stand naturally. Relax."

Edward did as he was asked, while the Official jiggled some weights about on the weighing machine, then studied the scale, and then called out, "Edward! Two and a half tons, five pounds and two ounces! Next!"

"Is that all?" asked Edward.

"That's all," said his grandfather. "Come along. Let's get you measured."

Again, there was a queue of naked hippopotamuses, and Edward joined it, at the end. But try as he might, he couldn't take his mind off all those other champions. There seemed to be so many of them!

"Grandfather," Edward asked. "How many hippopotamuses have entered the Twenty-Seventh Annual African Hippopotamus Race?"

"A record number this year," said Edward's grandfather. "More than have ever entered an Annual African Hippopotamus Race before. But don't worry about that. What's in a number?"

"But how many are there?" asked Edward again.

"How many?" said his grandfather. "Eighty-four."

"Gosh!" said Edward. "Eighty-four champion hippopotamuses!"

"That," said Edward's grandfather, "makes eighty-three you have to beat."

CHAPTER SIX

Sebastian

When Edward had been measured, his grandfather told him to put his clothes back on again, and to hurry, because there were still things to do.

"Oh, dear!" said Edward's grandfather. "It's nearly eleven o'clock. The numbers are given out at eleven o'clock. Hurry, Edward. No time to lose!"

Edward ran behind the screen, and, two minutes later, came out fully dressed, looking neat and clean.

"This way, Edward," said his grandfather. "Where's Sam? He'll want to come along, too. Ah, there he is."

Edward's father was still talking to the reporter.

"He's a real champion," he was saying. "I drove him here in our yellow bus. He slept like a top. Didn't hit a single bump. No, sir, not one bump."

"Sam," said Edward's grandfather, "no time for that now. We have to get a number for Edward."

"My goodness!" said Edward's father. "I'd forgotten all about the numbers. Come on, let's hurry!"

"What are these numbers?" Edward asked.

"Well," said Edward's grandfather. "When you get a lot of hippopotamuses in the water at the same time, it's difficult to tell one from the other. They all tend to look alike. And during a race, it's important to know which hippopotamus is which. Your school friends, for instance, will be on the look-out for you, and unless you have a number, they won't know which one is you."

"Humphrey and Tad, William and Jeffrey, Benjamin and Luke!" cried Edward. "Gosh! I'd forgotten all about them. I must go and find them."

"You can," said Edward's grandfather, "when you've got your number. Up these steps. Here we are."

Now Edward found himself standing on the *Official Numbers Given Here* platform. And just in time, too. It was eleven o'clock.

"Join the queue," said Edward's grandfather, "and when you've got your number, come back here. We'll be waiting for you."

"Eighty-four Official Entrants!" thought Edward. "Gosh! Will there be room in the river for all of us?"

"Nervous?" said a voice.

Edward turned around (he had been facing the wrong way, looking about) and saw that the Official Entrant just ahead of him in the queue was speaking to him.

"Gosh, yes!" said Edward.

"Me, too," said the hippopotamus. "My name's Barney. What's yours?"

"My name is Edward," said Edward.

"Pleased to meet you," said Barney, offering his hand. "Wow! Have you ever seen a crowd like this before? My stomach is full of the jitters!"

"Mine too!" said Edward, delighted to hear that someone also felt the way he did. Up till now, he had thought he was the only one with a jittery stomach.

"Have you ever been to an Annual African Hippopotamus Race before?" asked Barney. "I mean, even as a spectator?"

"No, I haven't," said Edward. "This is the first time."

"Numbers are now being drawn!" called a voice.

"Gosh!" said Edward.

The queue started to move slowly forward, but what was at the end of it Edward didn't know. It was impossible to see, because there were so many hippopotamuses about. Edward knew that if he stepped out of the queue to have a look at what was happening, he would probably lose his place and have to go back to the end of the queue again, so he stayed where he was.

"Do you think you'll win the race this afternoon?" Barney asked him.

"Gosh," said Edward, "I don't know. I haven't really thought about winning. I'm just going to swim as well as I can. Do you think you'll win, Barney?"

"Me?" said Barney. "I don't know. Everyone in our neighbourhood says I'm a fast swimmer, but I don't really know. I'm just going to do my best, too."

"I've been training for months and months," said Edward.

"Me too," said Barney.

"My grandfather has been training me," said Edward. "He was in the Fourth Annual African Hippopotamus Race. He came third."

"My uncle trained me," said Barney. "He was in the Sixth Annual African Hippopotamus Race."

The queue was moving along nicely, but there was still some way to go to the end, where the numbers were being given out. Edward still couldn't see what was happening.

Suddenly, down below, there was a great noise, and the crowd parted.

"*Honk! Honk!*" Edward heard. "Make way! Make way for the Mighty Sebastian! Make way! Make way!"

There came into view, travelling fast, a sleek, low, shiny, bright red sports car, with flashing silver wheels, and the windscreen folded down, and behind the steering wheel sat a huge hippopotamus.

He was the biggest hippopotamus Edward had ever seen, almost black in colour, with bright white teeth fixed in a hard grin. He was wearing a bright red jacket and a vivid green tie and white driving gloves, and, as Edward and Barney watched, he drove right up to the *Official Numbers Given Here* platform, brought his sleek, low, shiny bright red sports car to a sudden stop with a squeal of brakes, and then, with an easy swaggering air, climbed out of the seat.

"Who is that?" Edward whispered to Barney.

"I don't know," Barney whispered back. "Isn't he *huge*?"

"I'm the Mighty Sebastian!" announced the huge, dark hippopotamus, coming up the steps, two at a time, onto the platform. "My name is Sebastian, and I mean to win this race! I'm the best and strongest and fastest hippopotamus in all Africa, and the race will be mine!"

"He's an Official Entrant," Edward whispered to Barney.

Just then, an Official Hippopotamus in a white coat came up.

"Are you an Official Entrant?" he asked Sebastian.

"What if I am?" said Sebastian.

"If you want a number," said the Official hippopotamus, "you'll have to join the end of the queue."

"Sebastian doesn't queue for anything!" bellowed the huge, dark hippopotamus.

"Well," said the Official hippopotamus, "if you don't get in the queue, you won't get a number. And if you don't get a number, then you can't compete in the race."

"Who says?" said Sebastian.

"I do," said the Official. "It might interest you to know that I'm a champion wrestler and boxer, and the winner of last year's Annual African Hippopotamus Boxing and Wrestling Competition."

"Oh," mumbled Sebastian, and started to go off to the end of the queue, but just before going, he turned around, pounded his chest, and shouted, "The Mighty Sebastian will win!"

"Isn't he a boaster?" whispered Edward.

"Even so," said Barney, "he *is* the biggest hippopotamus I have ever seen."

"Move along, move along, please!" called a voice, and both Edward and Barney quickly moved up.

They were near the front of the queue now, and at last Edward could see what was going on.

Right at the front of the queue stood a big wooden barrel, with an Official hippopotamus in a white coat standing next to it. As each Official Entrant came up, the Official hippopotamus dipped a big wooden spoon into the barrel and brought out a tiny white marble, which had a number on it, and handed it to the Official Entrant.

"Gosh!" said Edward. "The numbers are tiny! No one will be able to see them when we're all in the river!"

"Next!" cried the Official hippopotamus in the white coat.

"Oh, that's me," said Barney, stepping up to the barrel.

"Here we are," said the Official to Barney, dipping the wooden spoon into the big barrel. "Number 51! Next!"

Now it was Edward's turn to get a number. Up to the barrel he stepped. Into the barrel went the spoon. Then out it came, bearing a small white marble.

"Number 65!" cried the Official, and handed the marble to Edward. "Next, please!"

"This way," said a voice, and Edward saw yet another Official hippopotamus was waving him forward.

"Get your singlet here," said the Official. "Have your marble ready."

"My singlet?" said Edward.

"This way," said the Official, and then Edward saw a long, low table, and on it pile after pile of bright white singlets, each with a huge number on the back of it, in jet black.

"Name and number, please," said yet another Official.

"Um . . . Edward," said Edward. "Number 65."

He gave his marble to the Official, who wrote it down in a book, together with Edward's name. Then he went to a pile of singlets, looked through it, and suddenly brought out, from right near the bottom, a bright white singlet with a big black number 65 on it.

"Try it on for size," said the Official. "Next, please!"

The singlet was a perfect fit. Edward turned around and looked over his shoulder, to see how he looked at the back, and there was the big number 65, plainly visible, for all to see. Edward felt very happy indeed to be wearing his singlet.

"It looks marvellous on you," said Barney, who was standing nearby. "How's mine?"

"Perfect," said Edward. "You look wonderful in it. I'm leaving mine on for my grandfather and my father to see. They're waiting for me. I'd better hurry."

"See you at the race," said Barney. "Good luck."

"Good luck," said Edward, and shook Barney's hand, and then off he ran to find his grandfather and his father.

But just as he was running to find them, who should he bump into but Sebastian, who was still standing in the queue, waiting for his number.

"Watch where you're going," grumbled Sebastian.

"I'm sorry," said Edward. "I didn't mean to bump into you."

"You've got your number, I see," said Sebastian, staring down at Edward. "Ha ha ha! Well, if you want some advice, you'll take it off this minute and forget all about the race. You haven't got a chance, little hippopotamus! I'm going to win this race. The Mighty Sebastian! That's me! Ha ha ha!"

And with the Mighty Sebastian's laugh ringing in his ears, Edward ran off to find his grandfather and his father.

CHAPTER SEVEN

On Your Marks!

Edward woke from his afternoon nap. For a few delicious moments he lay in his bed, cool and relaxed, as though today was just another ordinary day, and not the day – the long-awaited day! – of the Twenty-Seventh Annual African Hippopotamus Race.

He looked up at the enormous glittering crystal chandelier which hung down from the ceiling, over his bed.

Then suddenly he remembered.

The race!

"What if I've overslept?" he thought. "What if I've missed the race?"

He jumped bolt upright in his bed and quickly read the time on his alarm clock, which was right next to his pillow.

Quarter to three.

"Oh," sighed Edward. "Thank heavens for that."

He was so relieved, that for a minute he felt quite peaceful again. But suddenly he started to remember all the things that had happened to him this morning. One after another they came flying into his head.

The President! And how he had shaken his hand!

Being weighed!

Being measured!

Getting a number!

The cheering crowds, all wishing him luck!

The long queue of Official Entrant hippopotamuses! Eighty-four of them!

And then, while he was remembering all these things, there suddenly shot into his head something else, something quite different, and this time his heart really began beating fast.

Sebastian!

At that very moment, the door of the yellow bus burst

open, and in came Edward's grandmother and his grandfather and his mother and his father. And who should come in right after them, but Humphrey and Tad, William and Jeffrey, Benjamin and Luke, his best and closest friends.

"Out of bed, out of bed!" cried Humphrey. "The time has come for the race!"

"Gosh!" said Edward.

"We've come to wish you luck," said Tad.

"And then we're going down to the Zamboola River, to get our places and watch the race," said Benjamin.

"Where are you going to watch from?" asked Edward.

"First," said Luke, "we're going to the starting line, to see you start."

"And then," said William, "we're going to run to the finishing line, and see you win."

"I'll try my best," said Edward, "but there are a lot of hippopotamuses in this race. Eighty-four! And that includes the Mighty Sebastian! Have you seen him? He's the biggest hippopotamus I've ever seen in my whole life."

"Don't worry about him," said Edward's grandfather. "I've met his sort before. All brag and boast and can't swim an inch."

"I'm not so sure," said Edward. "He's *huge!*"

"Go and change, Edward," said Edward's mother.

"Good luck, good luck!" said Edward's friends, and out they all went, leaving him alone to change in the yellow bus.

Edward took off his pyjamas. He put on the bathing trunks his grandmother had knitted for him, navy blue, with a white belt. Then he put on his singlet, with the big number 65 on the back of it. Then he put on his new dressing gown. It was bright yellow, the same colour as the bus. And on the back of it was written, in huge black letters, EDWARD.

"Ready," said Edward, stepping out of the bus.

"Off we go," said Edward's grandfather, and off they went, down the hill to the Zamboola River, Edward and Edward's mother and father, grandmother and grandfather, all together, side by side.

All the way down the hill, the air was filled with cheering and shouting.

"Good luck! Good luck, Edward!" shouted the hippopotamuses and the elephants and the giraffes and the monkeys and the water buffalos and the rhinoceroses, who were crowded together, all the way down the hill to the Zamboola River.

"Thank you, thank you!" called back Edward, smiling and waving, in spite of his jittery feeling.

And all at once they were at the Zamboola River.

"What's that?" said Edward.

Right across the Zamboola River, from one side to the other, was something new. It was a wooden platform, stretching across the river like a bridge. But it was very low, only ten inches from the water.

"That's the starting line," said Edward's grandfather. "Specially built for the race. That's where all the Official Entrant hippopotamuses dive in from. See? They're starting to come out already."

"Good luck, Edward," said Edward's grandmother.

"Thank you for the bathing trunks, Grannie," said Edward, taking off his dressing gown. "They fit perfectly."

"Good luck, Edward," said Edward's grandfather. "And just remember one thing. Don't worry about anyone else in the race. Just swim!"

Edward walked along the platform until he saw a hippopotamus with number 64 on his singlet, and then he stopped. This was his place.

Edward looked around. The left bank was crowded. The right bank was crowded. Everyone was cheering. He looked up at the sky. Not a cloud in sight. Perfect conditions.

"Attention, please! Attention, please!"

Edward blinked. There, right in front of him, was a motor boat. It was cruising up and down in front of the starting line, and standing up in the back of it was the President of the Twenty-Seventh Annual African Hippopotamus Race.

He was speaking through a megaphone, and as soon as the crowd assembled along the banks of the Zamboola River heard his voice, silence fell.

"The Twenty-Seventh Annual African Hippopotamus Race," announced the President, "is about to begin!"

"Gosh!" said Edward, feeling his knees starting to shake.

"Here are the Official Rules!" announced the President.

"Rule Number One! No hippopotamus shall use a motor or any other artificial means of propulsion! If a hippopotamus does so, he will be immediately disqualified!"

A stir went through the crowd. Everyone knew that this rule had been put in because, in the Twelfth Annual African Hippopotamus Race, a hippopotamus named Alphonse had tied a motor to his leg, in a vain endeavour to make himself swim faster. Unfortunately, Alphonse's motor had got out of control, and carried the unfortunate hippopotamus over the waterfall, where he had suffered some nasty bumps.

"Rule Number Two!" announced the President. "No hippopotamus shall stay under the water for more than thirty seconds at a time. Any hippopotamus who does so will be immediately disqualified!"

Everyone knew that this rule had been put in to stop wily hippopotamuses running along the bottom of the river, which hippopotamuses can do, at eight miles an hour. One hippopotamus, many years ago, had actually tried this trick, but because he was under water so long, he didn't know where the finishing line was, and he ran on and on, and eventually went over the waterfall.

"Rule Number Three!" announced the President. "No hippopotamus shall leave the Zamboola River during the

course of the race, unless he wishes to retire from the race! Any hippopotamus who leaves the river and then attempts to jump back in and resume swimming will be immediately disqualified!"

This rule had been put in to stop hippopotamuses getting out of the river and galloping along the bank, getting up a good speed, and then jumping in again. Several hippopotamuses had tried this trick, but nothing came of it, because they were seen, and immediately disqualified.

"This race," announced the President, "will be watched at all times by the Official Judges and Committee, and their decision shall be final!"

Just at that moment, Edward heard a loud whirring noise. He looked up, and there, hovering overhead, were three large helicopters.

"What are they?" Edward whispered to the hippopotamus next to him.

"The Judges and the Committee," said the hippopotamus.

"They watch the race through binoculars. From up there, you can see every single thing that happens."

"The race is about to begin!" announced the President through his megaphone. "The signal to dive in will be the crack of this pistol!"

Just then, who should appear, running along the starting line platform, but the Mighty Sebastian.

"I had trouble parking my car," he panted, running up to Edward. "Where does sixty-six go? I'm number sixty-six."

"I'm sixty-five," said Edward.

"Oh, it's you, the little hippopotamus," said Sebastian, running into place. "You're still here, I see. Well, stay out of my way! I'm going to win this race! Me! The Mighty Sebastian! Ha ha ha!"

And he gave Edward a savage jab in the chest with his finger.

Meanwhile, the President's motor boat had pulled out into the middle of the river, where it could be seen by every hippopotamus on the starting line platform.

Carefully, the President raised his pistol.

"On your marks!" he announced through his megaphone. "On your marks!"

CHAPTER EIGHT

A Dark Shape

BANG! went the pistol.

Eighty-four champion hippopotamuses hit the Zamboola River!

All at the same time!

The crash was like thunder! It was the loudest noise that had ever been heard in all Africa!

Up went a torrent of water! Down it came, like rain, drenching the spectators on both sides of the Zamboola River.

And away went the champions, swimming as fast as they could.

For a few seconds, Edward didn't know what was going on. There were hippopotamuses everywhere. The second he hit the water, he had closed his eyes, and then he had opened them again, just to make sure that he was swimming in the right direction, and all he could see were hippopotamuses, swimming as fast as they could go.

"Gosh!" he thought.

Eighty-four hippopotamuses!

The most he had ever raced with was fourteen.

"Just swim." Edward remembered that that was what his grandfather's advice had been, and so that's what he did. He swam. He kicked with his legs. Over and over went his arms. Into his lungs, through his huge mouth, went enormous scoops of air.

Whoosh! Whoosh!

Meanwhile, the crowd was cheering wildly. "Come on! Come on!" they cried. "Hooray! Hooray!"

Over the Zamboola River hovered the three helicopters, their blades making great whirring sounds, while inside them the judges peered down through their binoculars, watching every swimmer.

One of the helicopters was fitted out with a special microphone, through which a hippopotamus was broadcasting a description of the race. Loudspeakers had been set up on both sides of the river, so that everyone could hear what was going on.

"Number 18 is in the lead!" cried the announcer. "Number 42 is ten inches behind, followed by 8, 60 and 2! A gap of six inches to Number 79, then 35, swimming well!"

But it was much too early in the race for anyone to be really winning. All the champions were still close together. And that part of the cool, blue Zamboola River where they were all swimming was blue no longer. It was white.

Whoosh! Whoosh! Whoosh! Whoosh!

"Number 22 is now in the lead!" cried the announcer. Four inches behind him is Number 28, followed by 3, 82, 41, and then a five inch gap to Number 65!"

Number 65!

Edward!

Edward was coming up to the front!

"There they go!" cried the announcer. "Past the one mile flag!"

"And here comes number 66! Swimming like a true champion!"

Number 66!

The Mighty Sebastian!

Edward couldn't hear a thing. He couldn't hear the announcer describing the race through his microphone and the sound booming out through the loudspeakers on both banks. He couldn't hear the cheering crowds. He couldn't hear his mother and his father and his grandmother and his grandfather calling out, "Come on, Edward! Look at him go! Hooray! Hooray!"

"There they go!" cried the announcer. "Past the two mile flag!"

Twelve miles to go!

Edward's father was so excited that his cigar fell out of his mouth.

"What's happening? What's happening?" cried Edward's grandmother.

"They're passing the three mile flag," said Edward's grandfather. He had a pair of binoculars to his eyes, and his mouth was hanging open with excitement.

"Can I have the binoculars?" asked Edward's mother.

"Just a minute, just a minute," said Edward's grandfather, too absorbed in the race to let them go.

"What's this? What's this?" cried the announcer. "Number 38 is climbing out of the river. Watch him! Don't let him jump back in!"

But Number 38 wasn't interested in jumping back in. He was exhausted.

"Too fast for me," he said, collapsing into a chair. "I've got a stitch."

Indeed, a lot of hippopotamuses were now falling back. One of them had bumped into the three mile flag, and had made himself so dizzy that he couldn't swim any farther. Another hippopotamus had got so confused that he had begun swimming in the wrong direction, and by the time he had realized what was happening, he was at least a mile behind everyone else.

And there were a lot of hippopotamuses who had made a very great mistake. They had started swimming too fast. They had swum so fast for the first three miles that already they were beginning to feel tired, and back they dropped, back and back.

"Number 51 has now taken the lead!" cried the announcer.

Number 51!

Barney!

Edward would have been pleased to know that his new friend was swimming so well, but, of course, he didn't know.

"Just swim."

Again and again he heard his grandfather's words. Over and over went his arms. Kick, kick went his powerful legs. Ah! Ah! went the air into his lungs, and out it came again. Then, he opened his eyes, and just in time too. He was swimming straight for the four mile flag!

Edward had just enough time to swerve past it.

"The four mile flag," he thought. "Ten miles to go!"

And in that same second, with his eyes open, Edward saw that the hippopotamuses in front of him, and to the left, and to the right, were thinning out. Not as many shapes as

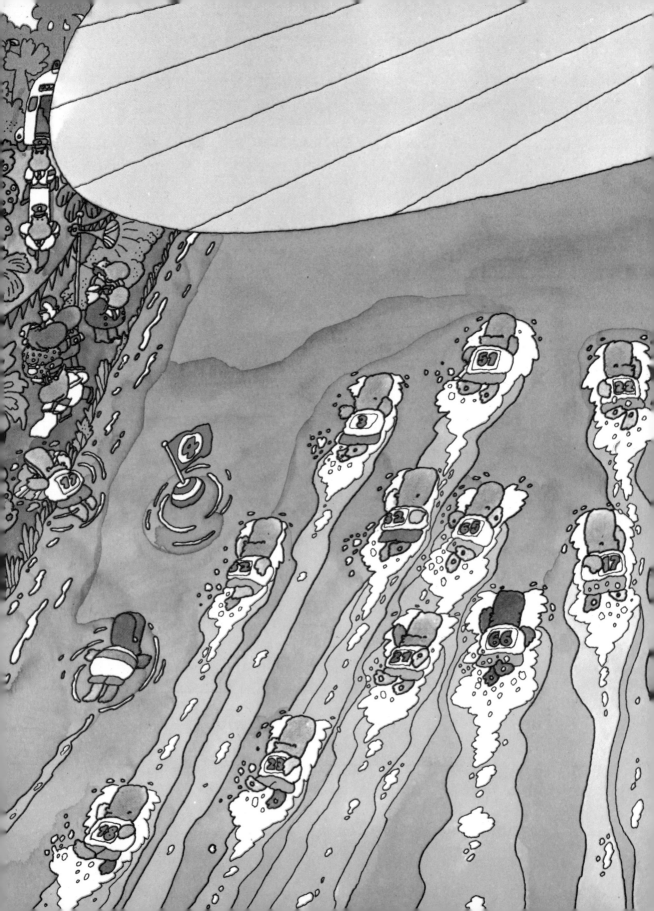

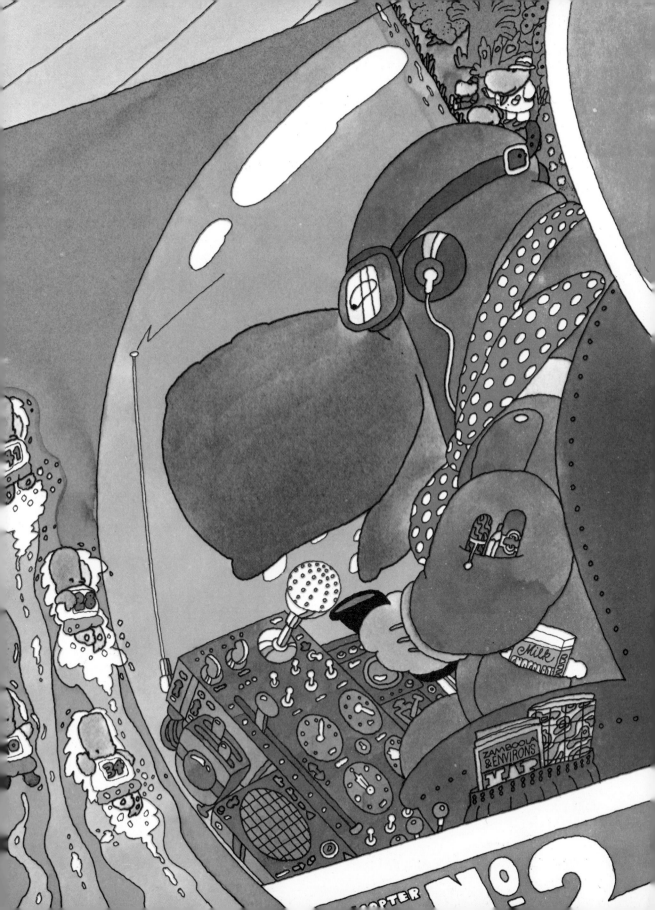

before. No time to think about that now. On he went.

But there was one hippopotamus who had a trick up his sleeve. His name was Horace, and he was Number 18. He was a good swimmer, but not a great swimmer, and he wanted to win the race more than anything else in the world. He wanted to win so much, in fact, that he was going to let his twin brother win it for him.

Horace's plan was simple. He had hidden his twin brother (who looked exactly like him) in the long reeds by the six mile flag, where no one could see him. He had given him a singlet just like his, with a big number 18 on it. The plan was, when Horace got to the six mile flag, his twin brother would slip into the river, swim under water, and take his brother's place. Horace would then swim under water to the reeds, and his twin brother, fresh as a daisy, would win the race.

Meanwhile, Edward was churning past the five mile flag.

"Number 70 is now in the lead!" cried the announcer. "He's on his way to the six mile flag! Behind him is Number 54, then 28, then 42!"

"Who is Number 70?" asked Edward's mother.

"His name is Frank," said Edward's grandmother. "Isn't he swimming well? Where is Edward? Can anyone see him?"

"He's coming along," said Edward's father. "Look at him go! That's my boy!"

Whoosh! Whoosh!

Past the six mile flag went Edward.

Meanwhile, in the reeds, Horace's twin brother, in his Number 18 singlet, was all ready to go.

His small bulgy eyes stared at the approaching swimmers, watching for his brother. And there he was, nearing the flag!

Into the river slipped the twin brother. Under the water he went. And there was Horace, swimming along, putting in his final burst, near to exhaustion.

"Here I am!" cried Horace. "Off you go!"

Down dived Horace, out of the way of all the other swimmers, and made his way over to the reeds.

"Ah!" he panted, when at last he had reached the bank. "Whew! What a race! I'd never win it in the ordinary way.

Ha ha ha! But Number 18 will win now!"

But Horace had reckoned without the eagle eyes of the Judges in the helicopters.

"Look!" cried a Judge, peering through his powerful binoculars. "Number 18 has crept into those reeds! Disqualify him!"

"But *there's* Number 18!" cried another judge. "Look! He's leading the race! He's swimming like a champion!"

"An imposter!" cried the first judge. "Announcer! Broadcast through your microphone that there are two Number 18s, and they're both disqualified!"

And that was the end of Horace and his plan.

But where was Edward?

Edward was fifth, swimming well. Every time he opened his eyes, another flag went past. He had almost lost count. But he knew that there was still a fair distance to go. And there were still shapes in front of him, so he wasn't first.

But that didn't worry him. All he wanted to do was to swim as well as he could.

The ten mile flag!

And only four shapes ahead of him!

"Come on, come on, Edward," he said to himself. "You can swim faster than this. You can't let your grandfather down, after all the training he's given you. Come on, come on!"

That did the trick. Edward picked up speed.

Whoosh! Whoosh!

He opened his tiny eyes, just for a second, and saw that there were only three shapes in the water ahead of him.

Whoosh! Whoosh!

But just then, when he was swimming so well, his arms going over and over, turning the water to white froth, Edward felt something strange. Someone had got hold of his leg!

"Gosh!" thought Edward. "What's happening?"

He turned round – losing valuable seconds – and there, holding him back, was a huge, dark shape.

At once Edward knew who it was.

Sebastian!

CHAPTER NINE

Over The Line

Edward had lost the race.

How could he swim with an enormous hippopotamus – weighing at least four tons – holding on to his leg?

Second after valuable second sped past, and Edward didn't know what to do.

Nothing that his grandfather had taught him had equipped him for an emergency like this.

"Stop swimming!" Edward heard Sebastian shouting at him. "Stop! I'm going to win this race!"

But Edward wouldn't stop. He still had one free leg, and both arms, and he used these as best he could.

Whoosh! Whoosh!

But it was no use. The three swimmers ahead of him were getting farther and farther away, and more swimmers were coming up behind him.

But what about the judges in the helicopters, with their powerful binoculars? Couldn't they see what was happening to Edward?

"65 and 66 are neck and neck!" cried the announcer. "Not an inch between them."

No, they couldn't see. Edward was finished.

But someone else could see.

Number 51!

It was Edward's new friend, Barney, putting on a spurt, swimming powerfully, drawing ahead. And just as he was coming up to Edward and Sebastian, he happened to open his eyes, just for a second, and at once he knew what was happening.

Barney knew just what to do. Out shot his arm and grabbed hold of Sebastian's bathing trunks.

"Hey!" shouted Sebastian. "What's going on?"

"Let go of my friend!" shouted Barney. "Let go at once!"

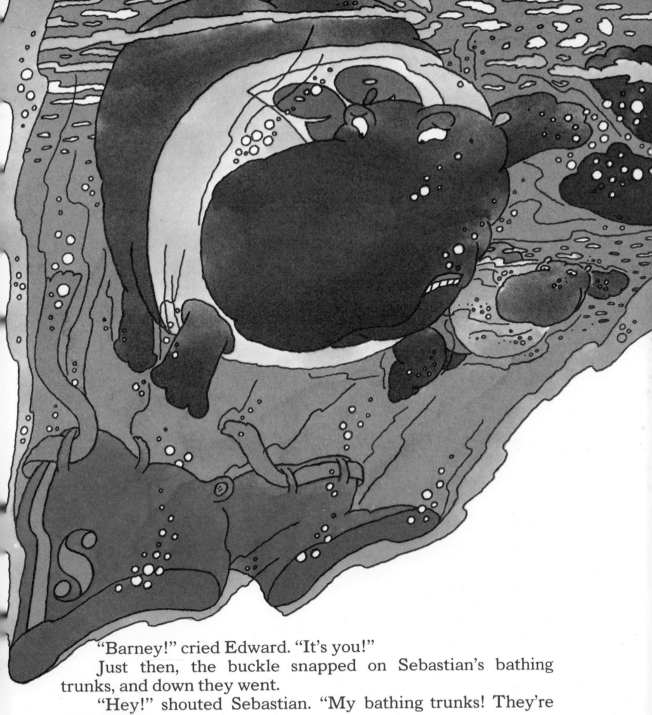

"Barney!" cried Edward. "It's you!"

Just then, the buckle snapped on Sebastian's bathing trunks, and down they went.

"Hey!" shouted Sebastian. "My bathing trunks! They're falling off!"

He was so peturbed that he let go of Edward's leg.

Edward, not wasting a second, shot ahead.

And Barney, seeing Sebastian's bathing trunks falling to

the bottom of the river, shot ahead too.

Only Sebastian was left, diving for his trunks.

But they were gone, never to be found again.

"Oh, dear," said Sebastian. "What shall I do now? I can't come out of the river without my bathing trunks, because everyone will see me. What shall I do?"

He was out of the race. He crept to the shallows by the left bank, and lay there, deep in shame, unable to get out until everyone had gone home. He was finished.

"An amazing thing has happened!" cried the announcer through his microphone. "65 and 51 have both shot ahead! It's fantastic!"

"That's Edward!" cried Edward's mother.

"And his friend!" cried Edward's grandmother.

"Only a mile to go!" cried Edward's father. "Come on, son! Come on! Come on!"

There was less than half a mile to go, and only two hippopotamuses ahead of Edward and Barney, who were swimming neck and neck!

Edward didn't think he could make it. He was exhausted. He had never swum so hard in his life. His arms ached. His legs ached. His whole body ached.

And that business with Sebastian had upset him enormously.

But, just at the last moment, when he thought he couldn't swim any faster, he thought of his friends, his closest and best friends, Humphrey and Tad, William and Jeffrey, Benjamin and Luke. He remembered that they would all be at the finishing line, waiting for him to arrive. He couldn't disappoint them.

Over and over went his arms.

Whoosh! Whoosh!

Kick, kick!

Out of the corner of his eye, open for just a split second, he saw grey shapes, to the left and to the right, but none in front of him, and that did the trick. One final effort, one more mighty kick with his left leg, with his right, and over the finishing line he flew.

First.

CHAPTER TEN

The Champion

"Edward," said the President of the Twenty-Seventh Annual African Hippopotamus Race, "you are the fastest hippopotamus in Africa."

"Gosh!" said Edward.

"Now, come along," said the President, "it's time for the procession. Everyone wants to see you."

Edward climbed on to the President's barge. It was a very large barge, with ten hippopotamuses, five on each side, each one holding a huge oar. The President gave the signal and they started to row.

Up the Zamboola River went Edward, happy and proud, waving to the crowds lined up on both sides of the river.

"Hooray! Hooray!" they cheered. "Hooray! Hooray!"

Behind the President's barge came ten more barges, and on them were all the hippopotamuses who had crossed the line in the Twenty-Seventh Annual African Hippopotamus Race.

On the second barge, right behind Edward, was Barney. He had come second.

"I wouldn't have won if it hadn't been for Barney," said Edward. "I would never have got free from Sebastian."

Two hundred elephants had lined up along the river, a hundred on the left bank, a hundred on the right, and as Edward went slowly past, they filled up their trunks with water and then blew the water up into the air, forming a tunnel, through which Edward passed, happier and prouder than he had ever been in his life before.

"The champion! The champion!" cried the crowds. "The fastest hippopotamus in Africa!"

"Only for a year," Edward thought. "There'll be a new